Who Will Guide My Sleigh Tonight?

Jerry Pallotta

David Biedrzycki

SCHOLASTIC INC.

New York Toronto London Auckland Sydney
Mexico City New Delhi Hong Kong Buenos Aires

ISBN-13: 978-0-545-11068-6 / ISBN-10: 0-545-11068-8

Text copyright © 2005 by Jerry Pallotta   Illustrations copyright © 2005 by David Biedrzycki   All rights reserved.
Published by Scholastic Inc. SCHOLASTIC and associated logos are trademarks and/or registered trademarks of Scholastic Inc.

12 11 10 9 8 7 6 5 4 3 2   8 9 10 11 12 13/0

Printed in the U.S.A.   08

First Scholastic Book Clubs paperback printing, November 2008

The job was too big for me. I needed help!

I had the sleigh. But one helper just wouldn't do.

I was looking for a team!

I tried tigers.

They played too rough. They almost ate me!

I tried mice.

They couldn't even lift the straps!

The penguins flapped and flapped.

Oops, they flipped and flopped!

The dolphins were really smart.

But — SPLASH! — they took me for a swim!

I loved the giraffes.

Oh! No! They got stuck.

I gave the skunks a try.

It was a smelly idea!

HOP! **HOP!** Kangaroos! HOP! HOP!

The HOP! presents HOP! went HOP! everywhere.

The turtles... were...

The cheetahs were too fast.

Snakes! Snakes!

too...

slow.

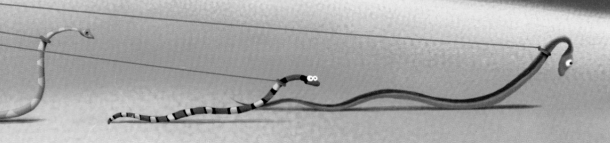

I DON'T LIKE SNAKES!

I tried rhinoceroses.

Bam! Crash! They smashed through a house!

"Don't even think about it!" said Mrs. Claus.

"Bunnies are for Easter."

I tried monkeys.

"Stop it! Don't look at my underwear!"

Then I had a bright idea!

Reindeer! That's it! They can do it all.

What a nice smooth ride! Yahoo!

Ho! Ho! Ho! Merry Christmas! Happy New Year!

Next year, maybe
I will try butterflies.